Creep, Eat, Surrender

Meghan Hoare

ISBN: 978-0-244-50256-0

To my Family and Friends

For a fellow biker and friend, Lee.
This is for you

INTRODUCTION

Imagine if you were, travelling to a country that you had never been to before. Maybe there was a job there or you were just going there for a holiday. Keep that in mind for one moment, now imagine, if a mysterious rock, was sitting in the ground, just sitting there, minding its own business, and, when someone touched it, they turned crazy. They started wanting to eat you, they wanted to make you their dinner. I am talking about the zombie race, the ghastly, evil, vile creatures you stagger the earth in search of human flesh and organs. What would you do for example, if you had to fight these creatures, kill them to save your world? What if you were the only survivor?

Zombies are interesting characters wouldn't you agree? The way they, stagger about, making strange noises. They don't make much sense. They were once real people, but these real people just died, and then, came back, only now as monsters. Strange isent it? Many people believed that zombies were just a unique horror character. Part of horror movies, like Dracula and Frankenstein. Yes I believed it too, and never thought it was possible. But I went through an extraordinary case where, zombies did exist. Where they were part of something so terrifying to the human eye. One country had faced this disaster already, and eventually there was a cure for this madness. That country was disease free, till another rock hit another country, and all hope was lost. I know, it sounds quite depressing, but believe me, it's a story! My my it's a story. We don't forget it.

My name is Professor Arbraham Reece. I am talking to all asking for help.

I haven't got much time. You need to know what happened, and how to end it all. Summoning all scientists and the world. Hear this story, hear me out. The infection has returned, and its hit London. Im seeing Zombies roaming around already outside the lab window. I cannot call anyone, the phone lines have been cut off. We are in deep trouble and we need help. The zombie disease has returned. We fear that, a zombie had survived the burning down of the game that ruined many lives, Zombie Creepers. I know that this doesn't make much sense but, I will reveal everything. I stopped the Russian Infection, I created a cure. This here in this bottle is a formula, I have named it Zombie 037. I am hiding in one of the labs at the moment, as the zombies, they've got into the Science and Discovery Lab. I have managed to lock myself in here, ive found that they've destroyed all of the formula, but this bottle is the last. I am trying to expand the formula to make more, but I don't have the equipment in here, its in the other labs you see. I am sending this message all over the world, calling for help. But this is aimed at Russia, you still have the formula we gave you last time, we are asking for your help. Send us the formula, send everything you've got. All the scientists, we need you. Im am trying to be as quiet as possible, any sudden sounds, theylle be breaking into this lab, and ille be done for.

As you can hear, there is a rampage outside and now in the building. I cant move. I am under one of the tables here. I fear my time will be up soon. I fear that most of the people of London are now zombies, I may even be the only survivor.Russia we need you, anybody.

Please, anybody. England will fall victim to this horrific disease. Zombies will rule if this carries on any more. I am begging you, on behalf of our great nation, to help us!

No! No! NOO!!

CHAPTER ONE

Once a year, a terrifying game is played. Its all about courage, bravery, determination, and most importantly, survival. Welcome to Zombie Creepers, a game that is set in a fake town, with high walls around it, so no one can get out. The only problem is, these aren't fake zombies. Captured from Russia, these were once real people, who were soon infected by a terrifying disease, that caused them to die, and come back as monsters. They had been discovered Johnson Wilkin,the game host, who wanted to create a game so deadly, that he needed something that would terrify the people playing the game. The zombies had been taken back to London, and placed in large cages, until they were put into the fake town. To think that, every man, every woman, every child, would be living a normal happy life, and suddenly, they'd become ill, confused, turning crazy mad, then kidnapped, and then they would black out, and not know they were being used in a game, killing people, ripping innocent people apart. It was the most horrible thought in the world. And they had no control over it.

The game was simple, survive the zombie apocalypse. If you die, you die. But if you're the last man standing, and all zombies are very much dead, you win the cash prize of a £10,000. But what these young souls did not know, was these zombies were the real thing, not people dressed up. The game had been going for years, and all the people died, no one had won yet. This was not an aired show, where It would go onto the tv, because Johnson was clever enough to know that if word got out that his zombies were actually real, his work would get shut down, and he'd end up in jail for it. That's why he moved the fake town away from the public, in a place where no one knew much about, expect for the people playing it. No one was aloud to support these people, there was no one watching the game, it was just Johnson and his crew. It was private, and no one knew the truth behind those walls. And the people that went to play the game, never got the chance to tell the world what it was really like, because they all died or they had become zombies themselves.

It all began when a mysterious rock flew in from the sky, and hit Russia. One man, one innocent man, had seen it land into the ground, and was so curious to know what the rock was all about. It seemed to him perfectly harmless, it just looked like a plain rock. But when he touched it. Something shot up through his body, like a lightening, making him jolt backwards. Nothing happened to him for a few minutes, until he started to change. He started to go crazy, he went mad. He started shouting and screaming, begging for help, claiming he was in so much agony. And then, he just changed, just like that. His body looked like mould, and his eyes had changed, he had no pupils in his eyes. He went and attacked more people, and from there, the infection spread. A fire accident then caused a science lab to catch fire. And all was lost from helping these people return to their normal selves. The hospitals were struggling, there was no hope, no cure.

Barbra, a journalist from London, was in the midst of it all. She was trying to get a plain back to London, but the pilot had been infected by the disease. She needed to get back home while she had the chance. Everyone was going crazy around her, she had nearly got attacked a few times. On her mission to find a way out, she had seen a scientist, who was already bitten, and about to change into a zombie. The scientist had given her a small bottle, a formula to end the disease, but more needed to be made, and he begged Barbra to take it to another lab, and to make more of the cure to cure the infected. The scientist changed into a zombie infront of her very eyes after she had made a phone call to a good friend of hers to explain the situation in Russia, and had then been attacked she could escape the scientist who had changed into a zombie infront of her eyes the moment she finished the phone call, biting into both of her arms. And then, she was whacked over the head. She woke up in the back of a van, and releasing how dangerous these men seemed, over hearing their plans and what they were up to, she carefully hid the little bottle in her trainor, and hoped it would not be seen. This van was taking her back to London, but not home. She was going somewhere else. She made to kneel before Johnson, who took his men into the fake town that had been built for the game, and she was thrown into one of the empty houses, chained to the walls. She told him he wouldn't get away with this, and she had heard everything his men had said. But Johnson only laughed at her, and left her there. Before long, she would soon become a dangerous creature.And that was where she spent most of her days, hoping and praying, that someone would understand, maybe a gamer would be able to set her free, and they escape, and tell the world of this horrid game, and put Johnson to justice.

When that would be, she would never know. But time was running out.

This year, there was 5 new recruits had seen the the game. Not knowing what trouble they were about to land themselves into. There was Paul Andrews, Tina Clyde, Jessica Heathcliff, Andrew Clyde and Barry Lewis. They actually knew eachother very well as a matter of fact. Paul and Jessica were dating eachother, Andrew and Tina were brother and sister and Barry was a friend of Pauls. And they all decided that they'd attempt to survive the zombie game. Tina and Jessica needed much persuasion, as horror was not their thing. Paul and Barry loved all things horror, Tina wanted to be a hairdresser, Jessica wanted to be a singer, and Andrew, he just kept himself to himself and stayed out of trouble.

Eventually, Tina had decided to join in. However Jessica still refused to participate. And the others went on without her. Paul, Tina, Andrew and Barry had set off to sign themselves up for the game, and just before they had, Jessica was worrying there was something fishy about this game. She had a friend who entered the game not long ago, and when the game was over, she'd never seen her friend to ask how it was. They'd just disappeared. And she feared, it could happen to her friends, and Paul. She never saw the people who entered the game around town, they'd just gone. She didn't want the others to join this game, something was telling her something bad was going to happen to them.

Jessica had stopped Paul as he was halfway out of the house, just as he was the others were about to leave in the mini bus.

''Paul...'' she grabbed his arm. "Do you have to do this?"

4

''Yeah! It's the most talked about game. Its so cool and so secret. We've waited ages for a thrill like this. Come on Jessica come and have some fun!"

''Paul, think about Rory and Anne, I don't see them anymore. Their not in their homes anymore, they've disappeared. Ever since they entered for the games, they never came back. Ive noticed it with others we see in the town. Its like the town is slowly loosing people!"

''Babe its not real. We might even win it!"

''COME ON PAUL WELLE BE LATE!" Barry called from the mini bus.

''Look ive got to go, its not too late to change your mind!" Paul took her hands and kissed them.

''No you go on, come back safe yeah?!"

''Of course!" Paul kissed her on the cheek.

Jessica backed away and leaned against the door, watching Paul jog towards the mini bus happily. They were so happy, cheering and shouting with glee. Jessica felt sick to her stomach. She feared, this would be the last time she saw the only friends she had left. She watched the mini bus take off out of the street and around the bend. She loved to see her boyfriend happy, but something was holding her back from feeling glad he was doing what he loved to do. She turned away and went back inside, resting her head on the door once she closed it behind her.

CHAPTER TWO

"ZOMBIE CREEPERS" , a big sign that was ahead of them. A gigantic land that was out of the way of London's eyes. It was located far away on a large piece of land. The walls surrounded what was on the other side the fake town. Old empty houses inside it, many barriers, ladders, balcony's. But outside of the wall was an odd looking cabin, and man standing outside of it with his arms folded. The mini bus stopped near the entrance of the game. And the man approached. He wore a brown overcoat and geeky glasses, and his stern look turned into a gentle smile as he approached the group.

''Ah you must be the new competitors!" he laughed, opening the mini door for Tina who sat in the back.

''Yes we're here for the game. Im Paul, this is Barry, Andrew and that's Tina!" Paul explained as he got out of the mini bus.

''Nice to meet you!" Tina smirked, raising her hand out to the man with a flirty look.

The man took her hand and kissed it, making the boys look on in confusion.

''My name is Johnson. And I am the host of this game. I own everything here. And I will guide you through the game rules, what you can and cant do once you are over the other side of the wall. After that, the rest lies in your hands. Come, let me take you into my office, and ille explain all!" Johnson explained, walking over to the cabin.

Tina was quick to follow him as the boys followed on behind. Andrew looked on in complete disgust as his sister stayed close to Johnson the whole time. They arrived in his office, a very small room, with many tvs where cameras in the fake town, all focused on certain areas inside.

''I will be watching you the whole time..."he explained, pointing to the tvs. "Once you arrive in the town, you will be asked to search for certain items that are located around these buildings. But it wont be easy. As you know, zombies guard this town. If they find you around their territory, well, youlle find out. But your not a team, its not team work, you defend yourself, you look after yourself, as if its all to play for. One of you will make it out alive, and will win the cash prize. The rules are this, you are not aloud to leave the game, if you get too scared and cant cope, I suggest you leave now. As you will not be able to get out. Secondly, you must not use the wepons on eachother, only on the zombies. If you find anyone who's about to become zombies, do not help them. They could pass the infection onto you if you touch them. Find all the items, kill the zombies, become victorious. Do I make myself clear?" Johnson asked.

''I have a question..."Tina put her hand up.

''Yes"

''Um, will the zombies try and eat us?"

''Most likely. They have not been fed, so they will be very very hungry!"

''And uh, are you single?" Tina whispered.

''TINA!" Andrew snapped.

''Anyway, if you would like to follow me around the back of the cabin, I will get you ready for the game!"

Tina nudged her brother in the arm angrily as she rushed after Johnson again.

''Dude what is she doing?!" he said to Paul as they walked outside. "He's so creepy and she's mad about him?"

Paul just shrugged his shoulders. Tina was crazy about any man she thought was hot. But she was really taking to Johnson. Around the back of the cabin was lots of metal boxes, and these boxes contained everything they needed to survive. Wepons, guns, bombs. Body armour, helmets. It was all here. They were dressed in heavy armour, with helmets, torches. In their belts they had small guns, and a rifle to carry around with them. They had no walkie talkies so they could not contact eachother, it was every man for himself.

Johnson then lead them to the entrance of the game, the large metal gates. Once these gates were open, there was a large wooden door, which took them straight into the town. A town they thought was the real thing. Once they stepped through that door, there was no turning back.

''Your fate awaits. Good luck!" was the last thing Johnson said as Paul was the first to walk through the doors.

Barry followed him, then Tina, who gave one last cheeky grin at Johnson, and finally Andrew. He flinched the moment the door was closed behind him. And right infront of him was hell. There were towering buildings and old looking houses around them, some that were very much rubble. There was a lot of mist going around, lots of things were broken around them. There was a balcony above them, which was like a watch tower to them. Each of them had been given a sheet of what they were supposed to be looking for, and what to be aware of.

The items were…

1 Silver Bullet.
3 Golden Chains.
2 Masks.
And 1 Bottle Of Blood.

These items seemed weird and didn't make any sense. But to the 4 of them,these were the items they needed to get to first before anyone else to win the game. But where, was the zombies? A siren sounded across the town, to let them know the game had begun. And they all went their separate ways. Now, they were not team mates.

CHAPTER THREE

The mist had brought a chill down Tina's spine as she walked alone inside a very old building, which she didn't know was just fake. The building was very cold, very eary, and she was convinced this was the home to one of the zombies. The building was completely empty, it was dark, is was creepy, and it made matters worse when she was about to approach a very dark room just around the corner. Her heart was beating so quickly and so out of control, they she stopped for a moment. To her the zombies were just people dressed up to scare her. They weren't nothing to be afraide of, were they? Taking a moment to relax her mind, she started to approach the dark room very slowly and very carefully. Her torch at the ready, her rifle close to her. Why did she join this game? Why didn't she listen to herself, to Jessica even? Whatever lied in that dark room was something nasty and evil. And it wanted her so badly.

Tina reached the room, and shone her torch around the room. But when she reached a corner in the room, something vicious, something vile and disgusting leaped out of the shadows, reaching out to her, covered in blood all over their arms. At first Tina believed this was a zombie, but as she quickly backed away still shining her torch on this strange being, she soon relised, it was an actual human being, not a zombie. Just a normal person, like herself. It was a woman, chained up to the wall.

''IM SORRY IM SORRY!" the woman screamed. "I DIDN'T MEAN TO FRIGHTEN YOU! PLEASE DON'T RUN AWAY!"

Tina paused, trying to catch her breath from the fright. The woman was a mess, her arms were the worst, there were two horrible marks on her arms that were oozing with blood. She was pale, her eyes wide wearing a white vest and ripped jeans and trainers. She was in tears, trying to get to Tina, but the chains were holding her back.

''Please help me! Please let me out!" she begged. "I need to get out!"

''Who are you?" Tina asked, steading herself. "You scared the hell out of me!"

''I know im sorry, its just I haven't seen another human since I got kidnapped!" the woman explained.

''Kidnapped?"

''You need to get out of this game. You need to escape. What you see. The houses are fake, everything here is fake. Expect for the zombies, their real!"

''What?"

''They were once real people, normal happy people, and then this disease broke out in Russia, causing this outbreak of madness, and the urge to kill. I was there doing a news report, and all these people were covered in blood, their eyes were a different colour. It all happened in a bank. Lots of people were dead and then they just got up like nothing happened. And then they started to take their anger out on others, ripping the living apart. Eating their flesh and organs. I tried to escape, but as you can see..." she pointed to her arms. " I got bitten by two zombies. And then I was knocked out, next minute, I was here!"

''But this is just a stupid game right? I mean these zombies are just made up. There's no such thing as real zombies!" Tina laughed. "Come on ille help you out of those chains. Or are you supposed to be like that for the game?"

''No please help me out of these chains. You don't understand. I need to find a cure, before I become one of them. They've chained me up because they know in a few hours ille be a killing machine. I need to get out, find a cure, and end this game once and for all. Please help me! If I don't get out, ille kill you!"

Tina was struggling to process what was going on here. Real zombies? No. They were just in horror movies. They didn't exist. She believed this was trap letting this woman out, she thought this was all part of the game, and something was telling her that this woman might make her loose the game. As Johnson said, everyone had to defend for themselves. She couldn't be part of a team, she couldn't help anyone. It was a look after yourself situation.But what if the woman was telling the truth, what if she really needed to be freed? The rules to the game were odd. But Johnson had clearly stated, don't help the infected!

''No, sorry I cant!"

''No no no no please! I have a husband and two kids wondering where I am right now. They were expecting me home from Russia. Ive been gone for ages now. They don't want to see me become a monster. Didn't you hear the news in Russia? Im the only one that can end all of this. I can make everyone become normal again, I can do it. Just please let me go!"

''Im not aloud to go near you, I cant help the infected. Your done for!"

''Johnson told you that didn't he? Yeah! That's what he always says. You believe him? He got me in this mess. You took me, he told me I was part of his game, and he wouldn't let me go. He's a mad man!"

''Im sorry I need to continue the game, and for your information, I think he's amazing!" Tina snapped, turning her back on the woman.

''NO NO! PLEASE! PLEASE DON'T LEAVE ME HERE! I NEED TO GET OUT! PLEASE HELP ME!"

Tina ignored the woman's pleas, and continued to search for the items she was to find.

CHAPTER FOUR

Johnson was watching from his office the tvs, he panicked that Tina was going to believe this woman's every word, and that his game would be over. But he let out a sigh of relief when Tina moved out of the room. He reached over to his walkie talkie on the desk.

''Maxwell, when Tina leaves the building, please warn Anna if she tries to persuade someone to help her escape again, I will kill her on the spot. Oh and I'd like you to help Tina, make the items easy to find. I like her! I, want her to win!'' Johnson grinned.

''Yes sir!'' a voice answered from the walkie talkie.

''I want cage B and cage C released near the Pink and Grey house, lets bring the zombies out!''

Maxwell was Johnson's closest friend and worker in the game. He was responsible for the zombies. He was the one that fed them and kept them in check. He was also responsible for letting them loose on the contestants and then trying to get them back into the cages the moment the game was over. A rope ladder was thrown down the side of the wall, and he climbed down it into the fake town to the Blue house, which hid the zombies. Inside were the most dangerous beings that ever walked the planet. There were 10 zombies in each cage, with 5 cages marked A,B,C,D and E. He reached out to his belt and pulled out two keys marked B and C. He had to be quick to get out of the way of the zombies, these had tried to kill him before. He quickly unlocked cage B, and ran out of the way out of the zombie's view, as they came charging out of the house out into the town. Once they were gone, he went back to cage C, and did the same thing. Once all of the zombies were released, he ran straight back for the rope ladder, one zombie charging after him, and climbed back up the wall, nearly getting his leg bitten off.

''I hate this job!'' Maxwell as he climbed down the other side of the wall.

Another worker, Karl, helped him down from the ladder.

''How's our feisty friends? Ready to eat?'' Karl laughed.

''Their temper has risen even more. Ive nearly died in there. Besides it was supposed to be your turn to let them out. What was Johnson thinking?!'' sighed Maxwell, pulling the rope ladder back down from the wall, wrapping it up and throwing it over his shoulder. '' He wants be to protect the girl in there!''

''That blonde?''

''Yeah. I think he likes her, and when I say like I mean a lot. So I got to risk my neck in there. If he thinks that much of her, maybe he'd should go in there, its his game after all!''

''Yeah well, what Johnson wants Johnson gets right?''

''Yeah well maybe he should show some respect. Im a close friend of his, now I feel like im being used!'' Maxwell huffed.

They strolled across to another odd looking cabin, that contained the food for the zombies. And the food, was not a pretty sight. These were human remains of the last players who were in the game. Arms, legs, brains, the whole lot sat in crates. And Maxwell and Karl had the stomach to cope with it. This was

15

their job, taking the human parts, placing them in bags, and carrying them out to the fake town. Throwing over the wall the human parts for the zombies. This is what happened to the past gamers, they became zombie food.

''Why does Johnson suddenly fall in love with a gamer anyway? His intentions are to use them as a bit of fun for the zombies. He doesn't care. No one has ever won the game anyway?" Karl asked, as they opened a crate containing human legs.

''I don't know. The man's gone mad. I think the power of owning your own monsters has got to him. He's never cared about women the day his wife left him. But this girl, just seems to bring out the worst in him. To me, yeah she's nice looking, but, why her?" Maxwell explained.

Maxwell was there that night that Johnson discovered his wife was seeing another man behind his back. Maxwell lived next door to Johnson many years ago, they were close friends. Almost like brothers. The relationship between Johnson and his wife was not great at times, it was one of the worst relationships that was soon moving to a divorce level. Maxwell heard many nights Johnson shouting at his wife, and she would shout back. Sometimes, one of them would walk out on eachother, and come back the next day to try and make amends. They constantly fell out nearly every day, and made up later on. Maxwell was not married, he preferred life alone. He didn't have much of an interest in commitment, getting married and having kids, it wasent for him. But hearing next door what life was like for Johnson, he was sort of glad he wasent in any relationships. But one night, everything got worse. An argument was now turning into a nasty fight. The first thing Maxwell heard was a something smash against the wall, it was probley something made out of glass. Next the arguing, loud and clear. And Maxwell feared this was not going to end well. So he decided to sort this issue out, and he went next door. Just as he was about to knock on it, the door flew open, and Johnson's wife, carrying some bags and suitcases, went charging out. Shouting and screaming her head of, telling Johnson that it was over. His wife could be firey at times, but she was a sweetheart underneath all that anger. But her true colours soon showed that night. When Maxwell walked into Johnson's house however, the living room was a mess. Most of Johnson's valubles, such as his plates with the royal family on them, and some expensive glass art statues, where now nothing but piles of glass and pieces shattered all over the carpet. Johnson was sitting on the couch, his hands covering his face.

''Johnson…''Maxwell began. "Whats happened?"

''She left me!'' Johnson raised his face from his hands in a calm manner. "She's been seeing someone else, for 5 weeks now. She says that im not good enough for her. So she's moving to Canada to be with this, handsome man named Arthur!"

''Johnson, im sorry!''

Maxwell was never good with situations like this, he didn't know what to say or do. Johnson was in a mess, and he didn't know how to make things better. Johnson seemed to have calmed down a little, taking easy breaths, looking around the living room, and seeing a mess it was.

''She's broken everything. Presents people gave to us on our wedding day. All my royal collections, just, gone!" Johnson looked at the floor. "I loved her Maxwell, I loved her very much. I would do anything for that woman. We never saw eye to eye yes I know that but, I really really loved her, and now, its all over!"

He picked himself up from the couch, and started to pick up the broken pieces on the floor. Maxwell began to help him, still feeling unsure what to say. He was surprised how well Johnson was coping, but he knew deep down the man's heart was breaking.

''Everything will be alright, im sure of it!" Maxwell said.

''You know what Maxwell..."Johnson chuckled, placing a hand on his shoulder. "You're a good friend, you know that don't you? You've looked out for me, you've been by my side, even now. I don't have many friends, but you've been like a brother to me!"

''Well..."Maxwell smiled embarrassed.

''No you really have, and you know what..."Johnson placed the broken pieces on the table. "Lets go to the pub and get wasted. What do you say old chum?"

Maxwell remembered how Johnson got drunk and soon forgot all about his wife. Maxwell was not a drinker, he liked the occasional beer or two, but Johnson was really drinking like crazy. Maxwell ended up carrying him home and putting him on the couch. He soon suffered for it the next day.

But as the weeks went on, something strange happened. It was a Friday night, and the news was on. Johnson was watching the news, he had completely forgotten about his wife, and had moved on quite quickly. The news report today was that in Canada, a deadly disease had broke out. There was video footage in Russia, everyone was screaming, running for their lives, being chased by these, crazy people who looked dreadful. Johnson was confused and surprised about what he was witnessing here, and then, his wife appeared with her new man, they were running. Johnson sat up, his eyes wide with shock. Then, his wife was grabbed by one of the zombies, Arthur was pushed away from the camera as he got attacked, and his wife, was thrown to the ground. She was screaming, begging for someone to help her, and then, she closed her eyes, and all that was shown was the zombies ripping her apart, and then, the video coverage lost connection, and was off the channel.

''What the...?'' Johnson gasped, grabbing his phone that sat next to him.

He started to dial in some numbers and then held it to his ear.

''I need you to come round here a moment, I need you to see something!''

Maxwell was round in seconds.

''You alright you sounded frightened over the phone? Whats wrong?''

Johnson had his laptop out, and there was a repeat video of what had just been on the news. Maxwell could not process what he was watching.

''Thats...''he pointed to the screen.

''Yeah!'' Johnson answered.

''But, your not, upset about it?''

''No! Im...'' Johnson started to laugh. "Im thrilled! This is fantastic!''

''Whats fantastic about it? People are getting attacked!'' Maxwell gasped.

''No! Forget the stupid people. These creatures have taken everything away from me. They've made him and her pay for they did to me. I owe these things, everything!''

"Johnson their dangerous! Their killing machines. You don't owe them anything! Are you out of your mind?"

"Maxwell…"Johnson looked at the screen with a massive grin on his face. "You don't know whats in my mind!"

The next thing Maxwell knew, he was travelling to Canada, to take the first batch of zombies. By then, after these zombies were taken, Canada was cured. But what was Johnson going to do with all these zombies, locked away in big cages he ordered. Maxwell then found that Johnson was planning something for these zombies, something that had never done before. Trickery, Evil, and Madness had been put into this plan. Maxwell found he was to build Zombie Creepers, a new game that had suddenly popped up in Johnson's mind. Johnson was turning into a mad man. These zombies had made everything better for him, and he wanted them to have their own home, their own sanctuary, where they would be safe from being shot at. He wanted to thank them, look after them. And whatever they wanted, he'd give it to them.

And from there, Zombie Creepers was released after a few months of building the place up. The game was placed on posters, there were no press, no cameras, it was just secret, but the posters were invitations to the game. The game was a success to Johnson, humans were paying the price and zombies were getting the glory they needed. It was sick, it was twisted. Johnson had become insane. Everything he wanted was ridiculous, and it was all to thank these zombies from taking the pain away from him. And Maxwell was part of it.

As the game grew over time, a new member joined. Karl, who was desperate for a job. And Johnson was offering him a good pay to help look after the zombies. Karl thought it was a strange game, till he realised the zombies were very much real. Johnson then made a threat to Karl that if he ever ran away from the game to tell the world what Johnson was doing, he'd shoot him on the spot. Karl had no choice. Johnson however treated Maxwell differently, calling him a friend, saying he was not a betrayer.

Maxwell and Karl had the pleasure of watching over these zombies, and making sure Johnson's orders were granted, with no arguments. But when Maxwell and Karl were alone, they would speak about how rotten it was and how twisted the game had become. And how they would never be able to change Johnson's ways.

That was when later on, Russia was struck with the disease with the next mysterious rock.

They placed the legs into some black bags. They swung them over their shoulders and walked back out to the walls again.

''If he wants her to win…'' Maxwell began. "He better work fast, because these zombies don't know the meaning of "behave". Their in a bad mood, and if you want my opinion, these people wont survive this game, no one ever does!"

They climbed back up the wall, and sat up there. Maxwell let off a whistle, that seemed to be something that the zombies had taken too. They had all charged like bulls towards the wall, jumping up in the air, stretching their horrific arms up towards the human legs that were stored in the black bags. Maxwell threw a leg down, and Karl did the same. They sat watching the zombies eat like wild animals, some fighting over their food with others. It was not a pretty sight when one of these were ripping open a leg.

''Its strange to think these were once normal, happy people. Now look at them!'' Karl sighed, shaking his head.

''Canada manged to cure them, their lab had not been burnt down like the one in Russia. Their working on finding out where these strange rocks are actually coming from, and finding a way to make sure they don't land on earth. But Russia cant find a cure. It looks like this time the disease is unstoppable. If they don't find one, it will spread, we could be next!"

''I sure hope not, I couldn't live knowing I'd become one of them if I was bitten. Just think that, if we became zombies, that, we'd be feasting on people, killing people. Who would want to live that way? Ha I know I wouldn't!"

CHAPTER FIVE

Barry had gone back to his list to remind himself on what he was looking for exactly. He seemed quite nervous about the zombies however, he'd never carried a rifle in his life. The wepons used in the game was described as not real rifles. They let off shots that sounded like a real gun, and the gamers were convinced that these were not real bullets being fired at the zombies. They were told it was rubber shaped bullets that when they hit the zombie, they'd explode red, and the zombies, if they were just actors, would pretend to fall dead. What Barry didn't know, was his rifle was real, and these were not rubber bullets, these were real. And the zombies were dying for real. The game was to convince the players that whatever they saw, whatever they used, were not real. It was clever how they tricked the gamers this way with whatever they used. The bullets they had were the only bullets that they had left, they could no reload. Once they used all their bullets, that was it. So they had to use them wisely. They had two more guns with them, but how they used them was up to them. Each wepon had 10 bullets stored in them. The rifle carried 20 bullets. It was how you chose to use them was they key. The bullets looked rubber from the human eye, but really, they were just dangerous things disguised to look fake. Besides, they all believed what they were told about the bullets being rubber were true. They were just worried about winning and finding the items. Being in a game was all about the winning, it was never worrying about how they were going to win, it was the determination and the bravery that pushed them on. Mostly it was the men that had that motivation to be stronger, braver and more willing to not back down without a fight. Not many women participated in the game. It seemed to be men who came across very arrogant and always saying they were the tough guys, but in this game, their bravery was put to the test, when a group of hungry zombies were running after them.

However, Barry had found himself in dangerous territory. He was a few meters away from a zombie who was feasting on a bit of leg that Maxwell had thrown over the wall. The zombie was a female, a very hungry female. Caped in blood from head to foot, eyes as white as snow. And pale like paper. Barry hid himself behind some old rubble from a fallen house, and raised his rifle. One false move would cost his life, he didn't relise his death would be for real. He didn't know that this zombie was the real deal. He wouldn't walk away a loser, he'd die one.

He aimed the rifle at the zombie, breathing heavily. Why was he so scared?

''Easy Barry!'' he whispered.''Easy!''

Being too confident, he accidently knocked over a brick with his elbow, which made a large crack as it hit the floor. The zombie, hearing this straight away, quickly lifted her head, dropping the leg on the floor, sniffing the air as she turned in Barry's direction. Barry flinched, quickly lowering his head behind the rubble. He was expecting a charging zombie, but she seemed to be wondering in his direction slowly, taking in many smells, but she had not smelt him yet. Barry kept his rifle close, his fingure on the trigger. His heart was racing, he didn't want to loose, this was all pretend. So he thought.

The zombie was getting closer, and as Barry raised his head to see where she was, she'd spotted him. He leaped up into the air, and started firing his rifle like crazy. The bullets were flying out so quickly, that she was hit multiple times in the chest and stomach. She eventually collapsed onto the floor, dead. Barry steadied himself, the shock slowly calming down. He kept forgetting this was all pretend, and it was only an actor. But it all felt so real. He ran away from the zombie, and continued his search, letting out a sigh of relief.

Beknown to him, he had just been close to being killed by a real zombie.

CHAPTER SIX

An hour into the game, and Paul had already been successful in finding the first item on the list. 1 Silver Bullet. He had found it in a wooden box that was sitting amongst some old bricks under the watch tower. He placed it in his bag that he was given for the game. He felt confident he was going to win this game, out of the four of them, he was the bravest and the strongest. Barry was his wing man, Andrew was the smartest, the nerd as he liked to call him, and Tina was just the pretty girl, it had always been that way. Paul took risks, he took chances, he was the leader of the group. He knew right from wrong, he was well educated in looking after himself and others. In situations like this, he took the game very seriously. When he was a young boy, he would play zombie survival computer games, he was made for this, he had been waiting for this day all his life. And now, at the age of 29, he was finally in that computer game.

He wished Jessica was here with him to enjoy this. Jessica was his life, he thought the world of her, he would do anything for her. He worshiped the ground she walked on, she was like a goddess to him. She was so sad when he went to the mini bus this morning, she didn't seeme happy for him, there was so much fear, worry, panic in her eyes. She knew the game was just pretend, but, somehow, she was petrified for him.

He had her worried face in his head, her beautiful blue eyes reaching into his soul, wanting him to stay back at home with her. He remembered those happy times, when they went out for dinner, the way she laughed, the way she would tell him her secrets, her deepest regrets, her dreams and desires. That smile changed everything. He was stuck in a trance thinking about her, and he soon had to drag himself away from his thoughts, and back to the task at hand. He walked out into the sunlight, and he saw Andrew from a distance. Andrew was about to approach one of the houses, he had so much determination in his eyes. He had the rifle aimed at very much anything that was in his way. This was the first time Paul had seen Andrew so focused, it made him smirk, as he carried on is journey.

Andrew had entered a very dark house, the grey and black house. Inside, it was just pitch black. The curtains were drawn, letting no light in. Andrew started to hear a very low growl, which kept his guard high and alert. He kept himself steady, the growling was becoming more and more clear to him. Something nasty and vicious was waiting for him. There were two rooms in front of him. One with the door closed, and the other with the door wide open. One contained his worst nightmare. Whatever room he chose, contained his fate. But could contain the items he was looking for. He pushed himself to go to the door which was closed, and he feared if he went into the open room, something was going to happen, and the growl seemed to be coming from that room.

He slowly crept towards the closed room, and gently placed his hand on the door knob. The growling had eased, and soon became deadly silent. Andrew kept his fingure on the trigger, and quickly opened the door. The door nearly fell of its hinges as Andrew swung it back, all he could hear was his the beat of his heart and his heavy breathing. All he could see now in the room was darkness. He chuckled, there was nothing there. Maybe one of the items were in this very room.

But as he moved inside…

CHAPTER SEVEN

Barry had entered the first house Tina had arrived in, when she encountered the diseased woman who had been chained up to the wall. He could hear someone calling for help. And he decided to investigate. He found that now, the woman was even more infected. Her face was strange spots appearing, and her breathing was very harsh. Her eyes were becoming blood shot, and now she was loosing it. This man was her last hope, she needed to get him to get her out of here, while she had the strength, because she was slowly starting to loose her mind, and she panicked that this could be the end for her. If he walked away now, that was it, she had no choice but to let the infection take over, and face it. It was the horrible thought about killing someone without her even seeing it or knowing about it.

''Please…'' she croaked. "Sir please don't go anywhere!"

''Im sorry I cant…''

''I know I know! But please, you don't understand what mess your in. Your all going to get killed. Your in deep trouble. Im not an actress, im a real human being. Please listen to me!''

''What do you mean your not an actress?''

''There's no actors here, out there are real zombies. Captured from Russia, I was kidnapped. I got bitten and im starting to turn into one of them. But I know a cure, and I need to get out of

29

here. You help me, I can get you out too. Just get me out of these chains!" the woman begged.

''Is this part of the game?"

''No no…" the woman shook her head, tears streaming down her face. "This is not pretend!"

''AGHHHHHHHHHHH!!!!!!!!!!!!!!!!"

''Andrew?" Barry turned his attention to the front door, turning his back on the woman.

''No wait! No where are you going?!" the woman yelled.

Barry charged out of the house, to suddenly find Andrew being thrown to the ground by 5 zombies, who were in a bad mood. They jumped onto him, Barry hearing the most terrifying scream coming from Andrew. He watched helpless as the zombies started to eat Andrew, his scream starting to fade away. He had been frozen to the spot seeing his friend being brutley killed on the spot. But to him, it was strange. He thought that Andrew would be told he had been killed, and would be taken out of the game throught maybe a door in the wall.But no, he was being ripped open. Barry tried to move closer to see what was happening, and he was nearly sick as the zombies charged away in another direction. Andrew was nothing more but flesh, blood, ripped apart like a dog toy. He'd been murdered on the spot, and it was real. It was really real. He wouldn't suddenly get up from that. Barry nearly fainted from the shock. He took hold on one of the railings by the house, putting his hand over his mouth in horror.

''This cant be!" he said.

He looked around, trying to see where the others were.

''YOU SAW IT DIDN'T YOU?!" the woman yelled from back in the house.

Barry turned his head to the front door.

''You knew about this?'' he asked, walking back in there. "You knew this was going to happen?"

''It happens to them all…''the woman snapped, looking even worse. "Every contestant ends up like that. They get killed, that's why they don't come out of the game. They are real zombies. You have to believe me. And soon I will be one too. Its too late for me! I needed to escape, I know how to cure the infected. There's a way, but im too late" the woman cried.

''I don't believe this!'' Barry gulped. "Zombies aren't real!"

''You need to get out of here! You need to get out while you can! Find a way to escape. And tell the world about this game. Tell them everything! End it!"

The woman started to cough violently, blood started to come out of her mouth.

''Whats going on?'' Barry asked.

''This is the start of it…'' she sighed. "I need you to do something for me"

She reached into her pokets, and pulled out a small pendant, which was the shape of a heart. She held it out to Barry, and a sad smile reached her face. She remembered when she was packing her bags, about to leave for Russia. She had her suitcases laid out on the bed, packing her belongings, and there her daughter stood by the bedroom door, watching her sadly.

''Oh darling…''she sighed. "Its only a few days, ille be back before you know it!"

''Do you have to go?''

''Come and sit next to me…'' she sat down on the bed, and lifted her daughter up to sit next to her. "There has been a discovery in Russia, and I have been asked to get the story on it.

You see, mummy's work gets put in a special newspaper, for everyone to see. All my hard work gets looked upon, im very well known for it. And so I have been asked to travel to Russia, it's a big opportunity, and I was the only one out of everyone in the office to get that chance. Me of all people! And so I cant turn it down, I get paid a lot, and well, I want to treat you and your father to a special holiday. Now what do you say to that?"

Her daughter chuckled.

''I want you to be good for your father while im gone okay. Go to bed when your told, make sure you eat your fruit and vegetables. No arguments. Ille be checking with your father alright. Just keep thinking about that amazing holiday we are going to have. The three of us eh?"

''Alright!" her daughter smilled.

''Good girl, ille be downstairs to say goodbye!"

She watched her skip happily out of the room, she was just 7 years old, and had the world ahead of her. She was bright, happy, she always did well in school. She never liked to see her unhappy, she missed that smile everytime she cried. She packed her suitcases, and then went to her black bag, packing her notebook, her camera and some pens. Once she was packed, she started to head down the stairs, to see her daughter and husband waiting for her. Her husband was very good at keeping things together in moments like this. He knew that his wife would be travelling to places, getting the news. Sometimes she would come home early hours in the morning, or late at night. He was very proud of her. He gave her a kiss and a big hug, and told her that everything would be alright here while she was gone. And when she looked down at her daughter, who shed a single tear, she crouched down to her, and gave her a hug, kissing her on the forehead.

''Keep thinking about that holiday!'' she whispered. "Keep thinking about it!"

''I have something for you!'' her daughter said, reaching into her pocket.

She pulled out a small pendant heart, and raised it up to her mother with a smile on her face.

''Take this to remember me!''

''Oh sweetheart...''her mother chuckled. "Your lucky pendant. Are you sure?"

''Im sure!''

She hugged her one last time, and walked out of the house. A taxi was waiting outside, and she turned around to wave one last time to her husband and daughter, who sat in her father's arms waving away, no more tears.

''Ille be back before you know it!'' she laughed. "I promise"

She jumped into the taxi, rolled down the windows, and blew a kiss out to them both as they taxi drove away. The thrill and the excitement of the travelling to Russia brought some much joy into her heart, but she didn't know, what was really waiting for her.

''My daughter gave me this as a good luck present, on my news report in Russia. It always makes me think of her. A heart of gold. I want you to give this to her, she lives at Avery Road, No.7. And I want you to tell her, mummy loves her very very much. And im sorry I never came home!''

Barry took the pendant off her as she started to cough again. It was horrible seeing her coughing up blood. It was strange.

''You might as well shoot me then…"she chuckled, looking at his rifle. "That is part of this, ridiculous game after all, isent it? Im going to be one of them anyway!"

''If I escape…"Barry said, looking down at the pendant. "You said you know how to cure the infected? Is there any chance that, maybe I can do something?"

The woman's eyes widened. There was suddenly hope and surprise in her eyes. The last bit of human kindness stood out in her face, before evil started to take over.

''Yes…"she nodded. "Yes you can. I had to hide it away from Johnson and his men, look in my left trainer"

Barry did as he was told,he reached over to her left trainer, and found a very very small bottle of blue liquid sitting between her foot and the inside of the trainer. He carefully lifted it out, surprised how she had managed to hide it in her shoe.

''If Johnson found it, he's break it, and make sure it would never work on them. I managed to store it in there when they threw me in the back of the van. You're the last hope now…"her coughing got worse, causing her to loose her speech. "Go to the Science And Discovery Building, give this to Professor Abraham Reece, and tell him I found the cure. Helle take it from there. Helle send a team here, with the police hopefully, and theylle knock the infected out, and cure them one by one. They should return to their human selves! The cure will then be sent to Russia, and wherever else needs it!"

''This bottle, this little thing?"

''Beleive me…"she chuckled. "Professor Reece is a man of many talents. Now get out here! Get out! Before I kill you!"

Barry picked himself up from the floor, the woman's breathing getting worse and worse. She seemed to be growling as she closed her eyes. Her body shaking violently.

''But what about you?!" Barry shouted. "This can cure you!"

Blood flooded out of her mouth as she opened her eyes, they were just white, her pupils had vanished. She was gone. All her human emotions were taken from her. Everything she could remember was soon brain washed from her mind, and now her brain trained to kill the living. She rose from the floor, and started to lunge towards him, but the chains threw her back on the floor, and Barry made a run for it. He had to find the others.

She screamed and screamed, her food was getting away, it made her pull harder at the chains. Her true zombie strength taking over.

CHAPTER EIGHT

Tina was standing on top of the watch tower, looking out at the fake town. There were zombies standing in different spots, they had fallen silent, full from their feeding hour. Blissfully unaware they had food walking around their territory. She thought the actors looked quite convincing, as zombies looked absolutely disgusting to her. She remembered when Paul had invited her and Andrew round for one of his movie nights, where he invited Barry and Jessica also. Paul had an obsession for zombies and zombie apocalypses, espically when they got killed with guns and bombs. The things that Paul was into, she never liked, and neither did Jessica. Sometimes, horror could be funny, but Paul's idea of horror was something horrible. The boys loved and took an interest in horror, while she and Jessica just liked to talk and gossip all night. They had no time for stupid movies that sometimes made no sense to them whatso ever. Horror was nothing to them, they had better things to think about.

She rememberd when it was Halloween. And how Paul, Barry and Andrew did everything in their power when they were young to scare Tina and Jessica witless. One time, Paul had pretended that he had been bitten by a zombie, and Jessica believed it. It had really scared her, and she didn't speak to Paul for a week when she found out he was messing with her. As

Andrew grew older, he was not playing pranks anymore, he had some sense, and that's how Tina never had to worry about being pranked by her own brother anymore.

She had seen Paul enter another house, and Barry running around like a headless chicken. He suddenly paused in his tracks when he saw her standing up there. He managed to catch his breath to shout out to her.

"TINA!" he yelled. "TINA!"

"BARRY I CANT TALK TO YOU!" she called back.

"NO I NEED TO SPEAK TO YOU! WAIT THERE!"

Tina shook her head as Barry ran up the stairs to join her. He was out of breath, beads of sweat pouring off his face.

"Where's Paul?"

"He's just done in that house. Barry we are not supposed to talk to eachother. Johnson said we aren't supposed to be a team!" Tina snapped.

"You don't understand. There was a woman, not an actress, she'd been chained up in one of the houses, she told me this is all real. They are real zombies. They..."he closed his eyes, taking a deep breath. "They killed Andrew!"

"Whats he's out? He's out of the game?"

"No he's dead Tina! He's a mess on the floor. They ripped him open. She said they were real. She's given me the cure to end all of this. We need to find Paul and get out of here while we have the chance. Otherwise we are done for! We need to move now!"

Tina looked on, shaking her head.

"Tina! Please!"

"Im going to pretend I didn't hear a word you said. Im here to win!" she hissed in his face.

She walked away from him, until he grabbed her arm.

''Tina you have to believe me!''

''GET OFF ME!'' she shouted, pushing him away, running down the stairs.

''TINA!''

He watched her run off away from the watch tower, sadness in his eyes.

''You stupid girl!'' he whispered.

When Tina had her mind on something, she stuck by it. She never listened, she was right, and the world was wrong. What she wanted, she got. She was told the rules, she wanted to win, and she stuck by it. Those childish days where Paul and Barry would do anything to play pranks on her and Jessica still remained in Barry, she thought that he was messing her around, and not taking the game seriously, like she thought she did. It took a lot of persuasion, a lot of time, and a lot of patience to get though to Tina, she was a tough cookie to crack. She was like that in school Barry remembered. She was one of those teenage girls you didn't want to get the wrong side off. She would get into fights and scraps, she would cause trouble, and everyone knew about it. She was very well know for being the girl that always answered back to people, and always ended up in the head master's office, spending a few hours in detention. Her school recorders proved she had no interest in her lessons, she'd rather gossip in class than take any notice of what she was being told. She never did her homework, she never did as she was told. And she found her school days more boring by the minute. She caused the most worst school food fight in the dining hall one day, and she was sent away from the school for a year until she could show some respect. She ended up not listening and was expelled straight away. She didn't have much education, but she could speak her mind, and she didn't care who knew about it. She was the worst child in the world, if she was president, she would ruine London completely. But growing up, she had changed slightly. She didn't have much of a temper, but a little bit of her childhood still remained in her, where she still felt she could answer back, espically at her brother, who was always the main target in the group. Andrew kept himself as far away from Tina as possible in school, he was being picked on because his sister was very much a bully and a loud mouth. He tried to stay away as much as possible, but Tina always found a way to rope him in to her troubles.

After hearing what Barry had said about her brother being killed, Tina hated Barry even more. If he was making it up, why would he say a horrible thing about Andrew being killed. She wouldn't have believed that Barry would say that about his own friend, unless he and Andrew were playing a prank on her to make the game even worse. Unless they had a trick under their sleeve that she didn't know about. Unless all the boys were ganging up on her to make her loose. Prehaps they were not playing by the rules. Maybe she should do the same, maybe she should catch them out. But would Johnson be watching. She noticed the cameras dotted around the walls, watching very carefully. What if he caught her trying to cheat? Would she be pulled out of the game? She wasent going to take that risk, if Paul, Barry and Andrew wanted to get into trouble and loose, that was fine by her, she would have a great advantage of becoming victorious, to put all boys to shame.

She wiped out what Barry and told her, and moved on, continuing the game. Her eyes were on the prize, she wanted to win, and a win she would get.

The woman tugged and pulled at the chains that bound her to the wall. The woman was getting restless, she wanted to run after Barry, and rip him apart. The urge to eat was driving her insane. She was using all her strength to break herself free from the chains.

''Oh...''Johnson chuckled, leaning over to the tv screen. "We have a new friend!"

Maxwell was standing behind him, watching the woman trying to break free. He felt guilty watching her, seeing what she had turned into. He remembered when he and Karl had kidnapped her, and thrown her into the van. It was something that he regretted, and even now, it made him feel even worse. Johnson loved the thrill when a new zombie was born. It was exiting to him, he didn't care the woman had lost her human thoughts and her human mind, it didn't bother him, he had no sympathy for her. He was just exited about the fact he had created another zombie. Another new pet as he saw it.

''How is my beautiful Tina, Maxwell?''

''She was standing on the watch tower, I caught her and the other man talking. And she ran away after that!" Maxwell explained.

''We have two more to kill, and she will be victorious. Our first winner. They wont last another minute!" Johnson grinned as the tv screen turned to Paul who was still in one of the houses, checking for another missing item.

''One of the men has found the first item, the bullet. How will I make the items more visible to the girl now?" Maxwell asked.

''Just be patient Maxwell, just be patient''

Maxwell didn't like it when Johnson's voice became low. When it became low, he knew something bad was stirring in that sick, twisted little head of Johnson's. The man's plans were awful and out of control, and all Maxwell could do was grant those wishes. Those wishes, he really didn't want to grant.

CHAPTER NINE

The morning was starting to fade into the afternoon, and the sunlight was turning into a dark, depressing, grey sky.It made the mood of the game eary. When the darkness took over, the gamers were in trouble. The zombies were closer wherever they turned. There was so much mist around, that the gamers did not know if the zombies were amongst the midst, ready to steal another life. But not one had been killed yet. Barry was trying to find Paul, who had already found the second item on the list, 1 Bottle Of Blood. He was on the verge of taking victory unless he found the 3 Gold Chains and the 2 Masks. He was leaving one of the houses, when he suddenly had to run back to the front door. There was a zombie, a male, standing near by the window. It was like he was sleeping, his head was tilted forward, and he seemed to just be staring at the ground, blood dripping from his mouth. Paul was watching the zombie from back inside the house, he tried to keep himself hidden in the shadows, as he watched him from the window. Luckily, the zombie had not seen him yet. The zombie was a horrible state to look at, his cloths were completely torn from head to foot and his body was a greyish colour from the infection. Paul thought it was clever how they made these actors look so realistic. He wondered if the actor actually knew he was in this house, but was just waiting for him to attempt to shoot at him.

''Lets make things interesting...''Johnson grinned, looking down at a big green button sitting on his desk.

Paul was about to take aim at the zombie, when to his horror, a loud, pitching alarm sounded, and the zombie, who was so silent quickly raised his head with a crack, he growled so loudly that he suddenly relised Paul's reaction to the alarm in the house, and came charging into the house, lunging forward at Paul. The alarm nearly made Paul deaf as he grabbed his rifle and started shooting at the zombie. But the zombie had got the better of him, he had snatched the rifle out of Paul's hands, dropping it on the floor, and pushing Paul onto the floor. Paul tried to reach for his extra guns in his belt as the zombie bit right into his shoulder. Paul let out a painful scream, and just about managed to grab his extra gun, shooting like crazy at the zombie with a scream. The zombie bounced backwards, taking the bullets. Paul was not expecting this actor to eat off his shoulder. He thought that maybe he'd have to touch Paul on the shoulder or something to say he was out of the game, but when Paul looked at his shoulder, the actor had left a nasty bite on his shoulder, that was oozing with blood.

''What the...?'' he snapped.

He looked down at the zombie, the zombie was covered in blood, it was a horrible mess. Paul was alarmed at what had just happened, he did not expect this. He was going to make a complaint. This supposed actor had just attacked him in a vicious way, a way he was not expecting. He thought this game was only pretend, he didn't expect the man to take a chunk of flesh out of his shoulder. He walked over the body of the zombie, out of the house, clutching his shoulder in agony. The pain was unbelievable. He thought he was going to faint from all the agony. He collapsed onto the floor, closing his eyes, wishing the pain to stop. This was too much to take in.

''PAUL!''

His vision was blurry, he tried to see who was calling him. But he couldn't make the voice out. He wondered if it was who he thought it was, but he just couldn't be sure.

''PAUL!''

He looked up. It was Jessica. What was she doing here? How did she even get in?

''Jessica?'' he whispered, trying to pick himself up from the floor.

''PAUL! PLEASE COME HOME!''

"Jessica?"

He tried to walk towards her, but he kept falling over. Everything was spinning, everything was not in focus. It was making him spin, loose control. He was loosing his senses. He was sure that she was right there infront of him.

''Im so sorry!'' he cried. "Im so sorry! I shouldn't have come here!"

He wrapped his arms around her, and collapsed in her arms. Sobbing, his shoulder bleeding even more. But as his vision was coming back to him, he saw Barry was actually holding him. Jessica was just a figment of his imagination.

''Where's Jessica?'' Paul sobbed. "Where is she?"

''She's not here Paul…''Barry cried. "She's at home! Oh god Paul we need to get out of here, we need to get your cured. Come on ille help you up! We need to find Tina!"

He tried to lift Paul up but he fell back down again. Paul was lite as a feather, but now, the fever was making him more heavier, more weaker.

''I need to see Johnson...''Paul snapped. "I need to complain about what the actor did!"

''He's not an actor...''Barry managed to get Paul on his feet again, and placed his not infected arm over his shoulder, carefully walking him away to safety. "Their real zombies!"

''Dont be stupid Barry!'' Paul shouted.

''Why would he bite you then?''

''I don't know!''

''Because he's very much real like the others are. We need to find Tina, escape, and get to the Science Lab. Ive got the cure in my bag. But we need to move now, we are the last hope! We can cure everyone. These people all around us used to be happy normal people, now their infected, their monsters, and they eat people. Andrew got killed, he got eaten! I didn't believe it at first, but I watched them rip him apart Paul! This is all real!''

Paul started coughing violently, blood coming out of his mouth as Barry carried him over to the watch tower, placing him underneath it, hoping this would be a safe place for now.

''And that's the start of the infection...''Barry explained helping Paul sit on the broken rubble. "You got to fight it Paul. Don't let it take over you! Just hang on until we get to the Science Lab over the wall. And this will all be over I swear!"

''I sure hope your right about this!'' Paul coughed.

''I need to go and find Tina, you stay here. Here take my guns, just in case!'' Barry said, pulling out his extra guns from his belt. "Ille come back and then welle find a way to get out! Just don't move okay, and stay awake whatever you do!"

''Just go and get her!" Paul snapped. "Ille be fine, just get her before something happens to her. Please Barry. Just go!"

Barry ran off. Paul was struggling to process everything Barry had just said. He didn't want to believe it. But all seemed to be making sense. There was a reason why the actor bit him, he wouldn't have done it otherwise. This was why he was feeling strange, this was why his vision was all over the place. Something odd was burning inside of him, an infection, a fever. He wasent sure if he'd be able to hang on until Barry came back with Tina. He just wanted to see his beautiful Jessica, one more time.

''Im sorry Jessica..."he sighed, shaking his head, a tear slipping from his eye. "Im so sorry my angel. What have I done!"

CHAPTER TEN

Tina wrapped her jacket around herself as the cold air started to hit her. The jacket was a present from her mother on her birthday, and when she had told her mother she was going away to play this game, she told her to wear the jacket as good luck, and that's what Tina did. Her mother was very proud of her and Andrew going out together as brother and sister to take on the game. They never did much together at their ages now, but this seemed a very special moment to her mother. She hoped that she could come home and tell her that she won. She was freezing, and was yet to find any more missing items. She was getting tired. She had just run away from 2 nasty zombies, had lost sight of them after quickly hiding away. She very much wanted to go home, but she hoped she could perhaps get Johnson's number. She had reached another house, but what she found at the front of it, made her suddenly collapse to her knees. She covered her mouth as tears started to stream down her face. The remains of her brother Andrew were still on the floor, all that was there was his legs, and his head, and his body, just flesh and bones. All his organs had been removed. Every last part of him was gone. Now it was all making perfect sense. Tina screamed as she cried angrily. This was something no sister expected to see. What had she done? Barry was right. They had killed him.

"TINA!"

A flash back had hit Tina, when she and Andrew were very young. When they used to play at the park together, never leaving eachother. They were more than just brother and sister back then, they were best friends. Andrew always said, when they were both 8 years of age, that he would always look after Tina, always protect her from harm, and never leave her. Those childhood years were years she never forgot, and she knew he never forgot those memories. But as they grew older, they grew apart. Andrew was always on his computer, playing computer games against Paul and Barry. He had an interest in science fiction and was a fan of Star Trek. And Tina, she was always hanging out with her friends with Jessica, they usually went to the pub to have a drink, always gossiping. Tina was of course the kid everyone feared. She had changed from being so innocent to being the worst child in the world. Nasty, cruel, and a loud mouth. She recalled those stupid times she argued with Andrew, the day she split up with her first boyfriend, a man that Andrew hated and knew was trouble. They had argued about it, and Tina had said horrible things that she regretted even now. She never listened to him, and that day she soon discovered, that Andrew was only protecting her, just like he promised all those years ago. Their brother and sister bond slowly came back after a while, but kept falling apart. And Tina had only herself to blame. She was the one that really changed, not him. He was still that gentle, charming brother who never broke his promises. He was the same with Paul and Barry and Jessica, he would do anything for them, he was a true friend, but he was also a brilliant, fantastic brother to Tina.

He nearly got killed for her, a memory that had haunted Tina for many years. She was very drunk one night, and had called Andrew late at night to walk her home, as no one wanted to walk her home. Andrew had got up from his bed, walked all the way to the pub, and helped his drunk sister home. She started arguing with him again for no reason, standing in the middle of the road, when a car, driving at full speed, came round the corner. Andrew jumped out, pushing Tina out of the way of the car, and taking the hit himself. Andrew was knocked out, and taken to hospital, lucky to be alive. Another day Tina regretted. The car had run over his middle fingure, and he had to have it removed. She hated herself for taking the mick out of him for not being able to swear with it. He had some broken bones and some bruises, but he was back up in a few weeks. But she knew he'd never forget that accident, and neither would she.

Before they had left for Zombie Creepers, she had ended up having another fall out with Andrew, and they had not spoken to each other since. Now she understood why he was so protective over her when she was all over Johnson. It was all coming back to her, it all made perfect sense.

Barry was running towards her. And he slowed down when he saw the unthinkable. Tina got up from the floor, and ran to him, bursting into tears.

''Im so sorry darling…''Barry sighed. "Im so sorry!"

''I should have listened to you!" she sobbed.

''Its okay! Its okay! We need to get out of here okay! Ive found Paul, but he's in a bad way! That's why we need to make a move, get out of here, and get him cured, and all these people. Okay, we need to do this for Andrew!"

Tina nodded, wiping the tears from her eyes. The thought of seeing her brother in such a mess made her sick to her stomach, it would be a memory that would haunt her for the rest of her life. How was she going to be able to tell her family about this? How was she going to tell her mother? What if she never came out alive? What if she died here too? It would destroy her family. This had to be the worst day of her life. The teenager inside of her, who didn't care, wasent scared, was willing to take on the world, soon felt sorrow and mourning, she wanted to go home. She didn't want to be the hero, it wasent for her, this game was not for her. She wished she'd never been here.

Paul was getting worse, he felt himself slipping away slowly. The pain was taking over, and he couldn't feel his arms or legs. He was starting to freeze on the spot.Inside he was burning, but something was making him slow down. He was getting flashbacks of the first day he met Jessica, at Andrew's 18th birthday party. He had known Tina, Andrew and Barry for a while, but this would be the first time he would meet Jessica, an enchanting woman from Northfolk, who had moved to London. He remembered that white and blue dress she wore, they moment she walked into the room. She golden hair shimmered, and her smile changed everything. Her lipstick, red as rubies, brought out the best in her. She and Tina would be dancing on the dance floor, laughing and giggling. And they would sit in the corner, and Paul always struggled to find words to say to her. He wanted to speak to her, but what could he say? What words could he use to not sound silly infront of her? Would he ask her to dance? Could he maybe offer her some food? What did she like and not like? Could he maybe use a cheesy chat up line? Barry and Andrew always shoved him in the back to try and get him to walk over to her. But Paul never had the courage too, till he eventually was pushed all the way to her table. An awkward moment he thought. When she turned away from Tina to look up at him, he was frozen on the spot, she had enchanted him, casted a spell on him like she was a witch or something.

''Would you like to dance?'' he remembered asking her.

''Yeah alright!'' she answered.

He took her hand in his, and led her to the dance floor, a song "Remember Me" played in the background, a slow beat, and they both danced slowly, their eyes met. Jessica seemed nervous, but she laughed it off, and after a while, something remarkable happened. Something Paul never thought would happen, they moved closer to each other. She wrapped her arms around him, he wrapped his arms around her waist, and she placed her head on his shoulder. And from that moment, Paul knew she was the one. And as the music came to a soft end, they kissed.

They went out for dinner at the American Dinner, they went to the cinema to watch a horror movie that even Paul was terrified of. All the memories, all the moments. They never left eachother's side. And here he was, dying. And she was at home, worrying about him. All her feelings were right, all her doubts were correct. He didn't listen. He felt like a child exited about being in a computer game like the good old days. But it was all mistake, and to him, this was the worst way to die.

He looked down at his hands, they were becoming pale, his viens were now red. Something was changing in him. It was the most horrible feeling that made him shake and tremble. He felt like his body, was not his anymore, it was belonging to something more stronger and wilder than him. It was like a

Jekyll and Hyde moment for him, the worst in him was fighting the best in him. And he couldn't control it, he was letting the worst in him win, because the pain was stronger, the pain won everytime.

''Hurry up Barry…''he croaked.

He heard a shuffle coming not so far away. As he glared up, hoping it was Barry and Tina, he saw it was a zombie, but to his horror, it was a little boy. Paul's heart sank, he was falling apart, and seeing a little boy in the same condition made him feel even worse.

"Can you help me?" he asked.

The little boy still had his human feelings, what was left of them, but the virus was eating at him. He had not fully become a zombie yet.

''Come here…''Paul said, painfully raising his hand out to the boy. "Don't be afraid"

The little boy shuffled along to Paul, his face was grey with blood spots around his face. But his eyes were still human. Paul took the little boy's hands in his, and told him to sit down next to him.

''Your having a hard time too eh?'' Paul sighed.

The little boy nodded.

''Your going to be okay''

''Whats happening to me?'' the little boy asked. "I don't feel so good"

''We are going to go to a special place…''Paul coughed. "A place that, will take all your fears away. Its called our soul, whats inside us. But our body's will be left behind, but we wont know what happens to them, because welle be somewhere else you see!"

''What do you mean?''

Paul sighed, wiping his eyes. The poor child didn't know what would happen next.

''Do you have a family?'' Paul said, still holding onto the little boy's hand.

''I got taken away from them. I don't even know where I am. I was on holiday in Russia, and then, these men took me away. I got bitten by this man, and, then I felt funny. I want my mum and dad! I don't know where they are?'' the boy explained. "Will they come and look for me? Will they find me? Will they take all this pain away?"

The little boy was remembering everything, replaying the moment he got taken away. He recalled the horrible ugly man that chased him and grabbed hold of him, taking a bite at him. He was so scared, so frightened, so confused he didn't understand what was going on. He wanted his parents, he wanted them near him to feel safe, but they were gone. He remembered Russia was nothing but darkness, there was so much going on around him. There were people screaming, running away from the people that were crazy and out of control. He saw someone being ripped open by one of the crazy people, that he had to turn away from seeing any more. There was so much smoke, so much mist as some of the people tried to shoot the mad people. But they failed a few times, and the little boy was thrown away into a van, and taken to London. He remembered he was made to stand in a line. One line was the normal people, but they were on the verge of becoming the mad people. And the other line, was the mad people. They had tried to break free, growling and hissing. Screaming, some attacking eachother in the process. The little boy remembered how ugly and horrifying these people looked in the other line. There was so much gore. He was then thrown into a cage with the other people, and was not aloud out for 7 days. Sadly, this cage was right next to the mad people, the ones that were trying to hard to get out of the cage. One moment they would be silent, the next, they were demanding human flesh. The little boy recalled the gamers who came. He could see them out the window, as the building he had been placed it was out of bounds to the players. He saw how some of the mad people, who he soon learnt were called zombies, were released every so often, and how they'd take hold of a gamer, and eat them. It was a horrible sight. One day, one of the people in his cage had turned violent, and had become a zombie already, and he had to be darted and removed from the cage, and sent out with the other zombies to play. After a few hours, the zombies who had been released would be placed back in their cages, and the next lot would be taken out for their fun. The little boy was sick of seeing the ghastly food these zombies had been given. He rememberd one night one of the workers in the game had accidently dropped a bit of flesh on the floor, and it had stayed there for days unnoticed, but the little boy was right near it, a horrid rotting smell making him feel ill.

Every human was different, the infection took hold of them in different ways as the little boy learned. Some would have the infection sitting in their bodies for days, building up in their system, slowly turning them into zombies. The infection would sometimes take over the human system very quickly, and it would take only minutes before a human was a zombie. But this infection sitting comfortably in the little boy was biding its time, but the little boy did not understand the horrid fate that was waiting to take its toll. He wondered if his parents were worried sick where he was. He just wished they'd take him away from this horrible place, so he would be free.

The workers had then let the nearly zombies, like himself, out for some fresh air, but this only happened rarely, it was the real true zombies that had longer out then what they did. They were aloud out for only 30 minutes exactly, until they were dragged back into the cages. The zombies had 3 hours out, then were placed back in, and then next lot of zombies were let out for their 3 hours. The little boy was so hungry, but he didn't want the human flesh, that had sometimes been offered to him cruelly. He was used to his fish and chips, his peas, his gravy. That nice roast his mother used to make for him. That's what he truly wanted. He wished he'd stayed at home, where he could be in the safety of his own home, his own bedroom. To go to school, to play with his friends like he used to. He didn't know anyone in the cage, no one spoke, everyone was so depressed, so miserable. Some demanding to be let out, to know what was going on and why they were here, and why there were placed next to the zombies. The little boy just wanted to find a corner in the cage, away from it all, and covered his ears from the noise, closing his eyes. He was sad. But now, finding a bit of hope when he found Paul, it made him feel that he didn't have to be scared anymore, he didn't have nothing more to fear, Paul made sure of that.

''I don't think they will kid…"Paul sighed, coughing again. "Im sorry!"

He drew the boy over to his chest, and put his arm around him, rubbing his arm. He felt like breaking down and crying, it was too late for them. But he didn't want the little boy to be alone, when the madness took over.

''You don't have to afriade anymore, just close your eyes!" he whispered.

CHAPTER ELEVEN

''We need to get to Paul, and find a way out. There's got to be a way out!'' Barry explained as he and Tina ran back towards the watch tower. "Ive got the cure to end the zombie infection, it can help the world, there's a Professor who's highly skilled that can help us!"

''Barry look!'' Tina called, dragging Barry back.

Before them, stood Paul, wobbling slightly. His pupils from his eyes had completely disappeared and now his whole body was grey, bloody and infected. And beside him, was the little boy. He was dribbling blood, his mouth wide open, and together they started to chase after Barry and Tina. Tina was the first to leg it and Barry followed, they ran, never looking back. The horrible sound of growling and screaming coming from Paul and the little boy. They needed to find somewhere to hide, to plan a way out, before they too were zombie dinner.

''WHAT DO WE DO?!'' cried Tina. "THEIR GAINING ON US!"

''QUICK! IN HERE!'' Barry grabbed her by the arm.

He dragged her into one of the houses, and quickly closed the door behind them. Tina hid herself away in the shadows, while Barry watched from the window, seeing a whole group of zombies running past the house. Luckily they were to stupid, and continued to run straight on, not thinking about turning the other way into one of the houses.

''Oh thank goodness!" Tina sighed in relief, catching her breath. "Now what do we do? We cant get out of here! They wont let us out! They knew about this, they trapped us here! And I thought Johnson was alright! Wait till I get my hands on him ille strangle him!"

''Just calm down alright. I need to think!" Barry started to pace.

Suddenly, a zombie out of nowhere, but herself, smashed one of the windows open, making Tina scream. Barry grabbed his gun, raising it at the zombie, shooting at her multiple times before she eventually dropped dead.

''I wish I never came here! I should have stayed with Jessica! Oh no what are we going to tell her? What are we going to tell her about Paul?" Tina sobbed.

The back door of the house dramatically opened, making Barry grab his rifle. But to their amazement, it was Maxwell, of all people.

''Who are you?!" Barry shouted.

''Im Maxwell, im one of Johnson's men. Im here to help you escape!"

''No im not trusting you!" Tina snapped. "You knew this was all real, this was a trap!"

''Ive been used and ive had enough! I want this game stopped the same as you! I want out! Karl is waiting at the top of the wall with a ladder, luckily Johnson hasent seen us yet, but we need to make a move, while the zombies are down that end. Johnson sent me to come and get you.I told him that you had been eaten by one of the zombies, in a space where there are no cameras.

He's convinced you've won the game, so he sent me to get you, but ive come to help you escape!"

''Can we trust you?"

''100 percent. We will shut this game down together, and Johnson will get what he deserves, but we need to make a move now!"

Maxwell was the first to go to the door, opening it slowly, peering out. Tina and Barry stayed close behind. Maxwell nodded to them, and they took off. A zombie not too far away had heard them, and was now charging, which alerted the other zombies.

''GO GO!" Maxwell yelled, as they ran through the town, all the way to the end where the watch tower stood.

Karl was waiting, shouting at them to hurry. He'd thrown the rope ladder down to them. The zombies were running as fast as they could, trying to get hold of them. Tina screamed as she tried to run as fast as her legs could carry her. She kept telling herself to keep going and never look back, telling herself she should keep fit. Those blood curdling screams made her shiver, she just wanted this all to be done and over with, she didn't want to be a zombie. She kept looking at the wall, looking up at Karl, the wall was keeping her going, but, she was convinced, that someone else was at the top of the wall with Karl. It looked, so much like Andrew. He was screaming at her to keep going, his hands going crazy, he was screaming her name.

''Andrew?" she gasped.

''COME ON TINA! COME ON YOU CAN DO IT COME ON!"

Her heart was going crazy, but his voice was pushing her on, and she found the courage and speed to go faster, slowly loosing the zombies.

Johnson, unbeknown to him, was smoking outside, not knowing what was going in behind the wall. He was waiting for Tina. But somehow, Maxwell was taking a long time. He had ordered Maxwell to get Tina, believing that Paul and Barry were officially dead. But now Maxwell had been gone for far too long, he was wondering if Tina had discovered their little secret, and was refusing to meet Johnson.

''Ille go and get her myself shall i? What's going on in there?!'' he snapped, throwing his cigar in the grass putting his foot down on it.

Maxwell had reached the ladder, he pushed Tina towards it, who started to climb up the ladder, seeing Andrew starting to climb down it to the other side.Barry climbed up after her, the zombies were getting closer and closer as Maxwell began his climb. Tina had made it safely over the wall, and Barry was nearly there.

''We did it! We did it!'' cried Tina.'' WE DID IT!''

Johnson unlocked the entrance to the game, and entered the town, seeing Maxwell and Barry climbing up the wall.

''MAXWELL!'' snapped Johnson. ''WHAT ARE YOU DOING?!''

Barry had made it over the wall, and Maxwell was almost there. Once Maxwell had made it over the wall, Karl pulled the rope ladder back up the wall, before a zombie got hold of it.

''NO! NO!'' Johnson screamed.

''Wait? Andrew? Where's Andrew?'' Tina asked, looking around. ''I saw...''

''What do you mean?'' Barry asked. ''I didn't see anyone?''

''He was calling me! He was shouting to keep going, he was standing with that other man. He climbed down afterwards!'' Tina explained.

''I think you saw a ghost!'' Maxwell smiled. "The heat here can get to you sometimes. You end up seeing things that shouldn't there!"

''No i…'' Tina looked at the top of the wall. "He was really there!"

The wind was getting up the moment Tina, Barry, Maxwell and Karl were out of sight. And Johnson was out to leave the town, when the wind slammed the entrance door shut. The latch on the front of the door fell across the door, making it impossible to leave. Johnson jogged over to the door, but it wouldn't open. He pushed at it, jamming his arm against it.

''NO! DAMN IT NO!''

The zombies turned away from the wall, hearing Johnson shouting for help. Unbeknown to him, the zombies were running straight towards him while he tried to get the door open, but the latch was tightly across on the other side.

''Damn wind!'' he hissed.

He had told Maxwell about changing the door locking system as he feared something like this might happen, and today was the day. He heard the growling and the snarling of the zombies, they were close. Johnson pulled out his guns from his belt. He started to shooting at the zombies, wasting so many bullets for too many zombies. He'd run out of bullets after a few rounds, but the zombies were too quick for him, and threw him on the floor. Johnson screamed and swore at the zombies, trying to get them off him, but it was too late, they were starting to feast on him, soon shutting him up for good.

At leaste they could have their revenge.

CHAPTER TWELVE

''We need to get to the Science and Discovery Building and give this to Professor Abraham Reece. Helle take it from here!" Barry explained once they were over the other side of the wall.

''Ille drive you there in the van!" Maxwell replied.

''What if Johnson catches up with us?" Karl asked. "Welle be done for!"

''Don't worry, the zombies took care of that! Lets go!"

They all got into Maxwell's van, and took off back to the safety of London itself. The zombies had no way of getting out of the fake town, there were too busy eating what was left of Johnson. Returning back to the streets of London brought so much relief back to Barry and Tina. They had survived the game, the first two to walk out of there, to tell the world their story. To really tell the story of Zombie Creepers. Tina was still concerned about what she had seen earlier as they drove to the streets of London. She saw Andrew as clear as day, but, both Barry and Maxwell, only saw Karl up on the wall all the time they were running, there was no one else up there. He was there, watching her run like crazy, his voice was so clear, it was no figment of her imagination. Maybe it was his ghost. Maybe he had come down to support her, to guide her.

They had travelled to the Science and Discovery Building, to meet the man that would change those who were infected lives forever.

Professor Abraham Reece was an elderly man with a high IQ. He was a man of great intelligence. This had been his job, his life, and he wouldn't give up for anything. But it was a surprise to him when Barry and Tina showed up.

''This is for you...''Barry began, pulling out the small bottle the woman had given to him before she changed over. "She says this can cure the infected, the zombies"

Professor Reece took the little bottle from him, looking at it with much interest.

''She found it...''he smilled. "Where is she?"

''If you are referring to the woman that got kidnapped for Zombie Creepers, im afriade to tell you she was bitten. And became a zombie. She's in the game at the moment probley causing a lot of havoc. I have a friend there also, he got bitten. But I was told you're the man that can bring them back!"

''You are correct...''he began, placing the bottle on the table. "Barbra was, a very close friend of mine. She was a journalist. And there was an incredible discovery made in Russia, and she went there to get all the news, and to make a report on it. She had contacted me, that a rock had landed there, and someone had touched it. And a disease had hit the person, causing them to go crazy. Out of control, wanting to eat humans. She had told me about it, that Russia was begging for help because the disease was spreading, even the hospitals were struggling. I spent weeks trying to work out a cure for this. The science department there had been blown up when the zombies got worse. She then told me she met one of the scientists, who was about to change into a zombie after being bitten. And he gave her the bottle, and told her to go back home to our lab, make more of the cure, use it to end the disease. I was their only hope. She said she'd be coming home straight away. But she never came back. The poor girl! I wish I had gone with her, but I had been very ill for a month" he sighed.

''We never believed her..." Tina began. "We thought it was all part of the game!"

''She was a good woman. And I know she wouldn't let me down. So I wont let her down either. Ille bring her back. Just leave it to me!"

The Professor was very confident. He didn't seem at all worried or stressed. He just went to work. He had a team of other scientists working with him, and they started to work on the cure. Barry and Tina went back outside to join Maxwell and Karl back at the van. And waited. They had every hope the good professor would do all in his power, to end the nightmare.

As the hours passed, someone suddenly appeared. Jessica had seen Barry and Tina sitting outside of the Science and Discovery Department, and her face dropped in shock.

''JESSICA! OH MY GOD!" Tina cried running towards her. They both laughed in relief and joy to see eachother.

''Hello Jessica!" Barry smiled hugging her. "Its so good to see you again!"

''You guys made it out! You actually got out of the game!?"

''Sort of!" Tina said, looking up at Barry sadly. "I think you need to sit down a minute Jessica. We need to explain something to you!"

''What do you mean? I need to sit down? This is amazing? Wait where's Paul and Andrew?"

''Thats what we need to tell you!" Barry added as Jessica took a seat at the stairs.

''Who's these guys?" Jessica pointed to Maxwell and Karl standing by the van.

''This is Maxwell. He helped us escape, and this is Karl, their both workers in the game!" Tina explained.

''Helped you escape? Im sure that's not what happens in the game. There's no way of..."

''Jessica, the game was, not as we thought. We were tricked, we were trapped. Andrew was ripped apart and..." Tina closed her eyes. "Paul got turned into a zombie!"

''What are you talking about? Don't be silly? Zombies aren't real!" Jessica laughed. "Do you believe them?" she looked up at Maxwell and Karl, who were not laughing. "You've got to be kidding me!"

''Welle take you to the game and you can see for yourself Jessica, he's one of them. But don't worry, there's a man in this building that is going to bring them all back to normal!" Barry added. "Helle come back, helle be fine I swear!"

''What will they do to him?" Jessica said.

''They will all be darted, and will be injected with the formula. Then this will sent off to Russia before the disease spreads around the world. Then, the disease will be over, and everything will be back to normal again!" Maxwell replied. "The quicker the formula gets to those, the quicker the disease will stop spreading!"

''And you've seen all this!"

''Ive been part of the game for many years miss, I have seen things that have should not happen. Johnson was a bad man, a man that deserved what he got. He was messed up in the head,

64

he thought he could keep the game going for a long as he could. Luckily this time we had smart people to work out what was going on" Maxwell nodded to Tina and Barry.

Jessica shook her head, processing all of this was not easy. Her boyfriend had become a vicious killing machine, Barry and Tina were the first ever contestants to walk away from the game. And there was a zombie apocalypse brewing, all in one day.

CHAPTER THIRTEEN

7pm, and the Professor had finally appeared, with a few crates of the cure in some more bigger bottles. He had managed to expand the formula, making more of it to be used, and had stored more in the lab to be taken to Russia. Taking their dart guns with them, Barry, Tina and Jessica had tagged on to help. They drove back to the game venue, and with the help of some of the Professor's fellow scientists. Some stood on top of the walls to take aim at the zombies from above, and some, like Maxwell, Karl and Barry, charged into the fake town, and began to dart the zombies. Barry was the one to take Paul down, and it wasent an easy job. Maxwell stored some of the zombies in his van, and some of the scientists took more in their verchiles. Jessica never left Paul's side, even though he looked a mess, she hoped he would come back to her, the man he was before. It had been the longest adventure of their lives, and now, it was time to end the terror Zombie Creepers had brought to them. All the infected where brought back to the lab one by one, there must have been a 100 infected people who had transformed lying in the lab. They were all injected with the cure formula, and after 10 whole minutes, the infected, where back to their normal healthy selves. The colours were coming back into their cheeks. They were breathing again, every man and woman were opening their eyes, lying on the lab floor, confused at first, but thankful they were alive. Jessica never let go of Paul the moment he opened his eyes, they laughed as they hugged each other, he was so happy she was there will him, she was no figment of his imagination anymore. The little boy had been lying beside him, and Paul pulled him over for a hug when he woke up.

''I told you everything was going to be alright!'' he told the boy.

The professor helped Barbra off the floor when she awoke, tears starting to form in her eyes the moment she knew where she was, and what had just happened. The happiness that the cure had safely got to the Professor was enough to make Barbra cry with joy. The people hugged eachother, even if they didn't know eachother, it was just great to feel alive and normal again. When everyone returned home, Paul, Jessica, Tina and Barry had left the Science and Discovery Building, after saying their farewells to the Barbra and the Professor, both eternally grateful for Barry and Tina's bravery and courage.

''Well Professor, you did it!'' Barbra laughed, putting her hand on the Professor's shoulder.

''Im just glad everyone's alright. It may take them a while to get over everything, but the disease is fully out of their system! And you young lady, I think someone's waiting outside for you!''

Barbra looked at him in confusion at first, till she could see from the glass doors someone waiting down the bottom of the stairs. It was, her daughter. Barbra ran out of the lab, down to the glass doors, and flew off the stairs down to her daughter, picking her up into a big hug.

''Oh sweetheart…"she cried, kissing her forehead."Oh im so happy! Oh my goodness!"

Her husband was standing watching very proudly, emotional himself, and wrapped her arms around him, with her daughter still close by. Paul, Jessica, Tina and Barry were watching this with emotional smiles. Barry looked down at his pocket, he felt something small in his hand, in the shape of a heart, and it brought a gentle smile to his face. He approached the little girl, patting her on the shoulder. She looked at him, her eyes sparkling as she laughed from the excitement of seeing her mother again.

''I think this belongs to you…"he grinned, holding the little pendant heart up to her.

''Thankyou mister!" the little girl said, taking the pendant gently from him.

''Your very welcome!"

Barry stood back up, and gave one last wave to the little girl and Barbra, as the three of them walked away into the shadows, heading back home.

''Lets plan that holiday shall we?!" they heard Barbra laugh.

''Who's up for some pizza back at my place?" Paul called.

''I say yes to that!" Tina put her hand up laughing. "Lets go!"

She put her arm around Barry as they walked off into the distance, but Paul and Jessica, still stayed by the stairs.

''I cant believe I saw Andrew up on that wall. He looked so real. But it was just a ghost!" Tina sighed.

''He must be very proud of you, he must be the most luckiest man in the world to have a sister like you, we are all proud of you, you know that?" Barry rubbed her back as they carried on walking.

''I don't know how to tell my family…"Tina sobbed, it finally getting to her. "Its going to destroy mum. I don't think im ready to tell her yet!"

''Welle go together!" Barry said.

''Yeah!"

Paul looked up at the stars in the sky, a smile reaching across his face. Something warm and happy inside of him, was helping him build up to a very special moment, that he felt was the right moment, to admit his real true feelings for Jessica.

''What are you smiling about?" Jessica smirked, nudging him in the shoulder. "Come on tell me!"

''Jessica, before we go…"he said. "I cant tell you how much I missed you!"

''And I missed you too sweetie!" Jessica smiled, cupping his cheeks with her hands.

''So…"he knelt down on one knee, making Jessica gasp in shock.

Tina and Barry had turned to see if Paul and Jessica were behind them, but they paused in shock when they saw what was going on. And then, snow flakes began to fall upon them. This was something magical, something so unexpected, like being in a fairy tale.

The night Paul didn't have any words to say to Jessica when they met for the first time, he finally had the words now, the courage to finally ask her a question.

''Jessica, I haven't got a ring on me right now!" he chuckled, making Jessican laugh. "But, will you, make me a very happy man, and marry me?" he asked.

''SAY YES!" Tina cried from a distance. "SAY YES SAY YES!"

''Yes!'' Jessica answered.

Paul grabbed her and drew her into a kiss, Tina and Barry cheered and ran over to them, giving them both a hug. The true, real survivors of Zombie Creepers, the people to tell the tale of the game, where no one came out alive, but them. It became a news story, the whole world learnt of the terrible trap that was hidden in London, that made gamers who loved horror and zombie, come to take on the challenge, never to know that they would never come out alive again. Johnson's name was not forgotten, nor was Zombie Creepers, it would take a while to forget the horrors he caused, but they wouldn't forget what he had done, what he had caused. But London would learn to forget those who caused such horrors like these.

Karl wrote a book on it, telling about his life working for Johnson and being a worker in the game, revealing all. And Maxwell made a new life for himself, and moved to Italy. Paul and Jessica got married on Christmas Day and spent the honeymoon away in Ibiza. It was fair to say that they lived happily ever after, and zombies to Paul was just a distant memory. He was no longer a boy playing computer games, he was more interested in being a good husband to Jessica, who he loved and worshipped for the rest of his life.And Tina finally got her job as a hairdresser, owning her own shop, with the help of her mother. She finally forfilled all of her dreams, and it was all in the memory of Andrew.

She with the help of Barry, Paul and Jessica, had found the courage to tell her family on the day they had escaped the game,about Andrew's death in the game, something that destroyed her mother competly, and her father completely heartbroken. Andrew's funeral was a day that celebrated

Andrew's kindess, gentleness, and bravery, and remembering Andrew was the man he was before he entered the game. When he was buried, Tina had seen Andrew's ghost once again, standing by the trees, watching, with a very proud smile on his face. It made her smile back at him. He walked amongst the trees soon vanishing. Her mother appeared by her side, seeing Tina smiling looking on at the trees, tears forming in her eyes.

''Are you alright love?" she said, placing a hand on her shoulder.

''Yes mum..." Tina turned to her. "Andrew was here. He was watching. He's happy mum, he was standing there smiling at us. He's with us!"

''Oh love, I know he is!"

They both hugged eachother, letting all their emotions out.

As for Barry took an interest in science, and joined Professor Reece and his team at the Science and Discovery Building. The formula cure became a huge fascination to him, and he wanted to learn more about it. He actually ended up helping to make more of it to send out to Russia. He soon became very famous as a scientist, soon making history with his new discoveries, which was mostly on medicines to cure the weak and ill.

The formula cure was sent to Russia, and the infected were cured there too. A new Science Lab was being built there, and the rock that started it all, was burnt and officially destroyed. Russia soon forgot about it all, and continued there life. The scientists were then working on ways to stop another rock from falling, to make sure that they were able to stop the any more mysterious rocks from falling into earth. They were working on find the source on where the rocks were coming from, something that Barry took part in proudly.

And the little boy, he was finally reunited with his parents, with the help of Paul, who had offered to help him find them. The little boy was exited to tell his parents about his crazy journey, and how Paul had looked after him in his darkest hour.

The fake town, the game venue, was burnt to the ground by Paul and Barry and Karl, in memory of Andrew. It was a proud day to see the town fall to pieces, and the wall was finally burnt to the ground, like the place had never existed. They drank some beer, sitting on top of the van, watching the place fall apart.

''Do you think Andrew's watching us up there?'' Barry asked looking up at the sky.

''I think he'd be happy to see this place go!'' Paul laughed.

And Zombie Creepers, was just a distant memory.

CHAPTER FOURTEEN

What was left of the Zombie Creepers venue was just broken rubble, there was nothing left. Everything was dull and black and depressing. Soon, something new and exiting was going to be built there to take away the bad memories. The sun was starting to set upon the land. The sound of the zombie's screams and growls still haunted the air, it was like they could still be heard. Amongst some rubble, something try to break free. A low growl was hurtling through the rubble, and a hand suddenly appeared, grasping the air. It was a pale grey, the viens red. It then grabbed hold of the broken rubble, pulling itself up. Johnson was pulling himself up from the rubble, his cloths covered in blood and dust. His face full of spots, he had no pupils in his eyes, he was dribbling blood, his cloths torn. One of the cameras had managed to survive the fire, and was still filming. Johnson had caught sight of it, he staggered towards it, growling, looking down at it with his haunting eyes.

''ITS NOT OVER!'' he growled, as the last of his human speech remained for now.

He started to stagger away from it, the walls not guarding him anymore. He was heading straight in the direction of the streets of London.

The dead, will walk, again.

Lightning Source UK Ltd.
Milton Keynes UK
UKHW050240270422
402079UK00015B/1032

9 780244 502560